Juliet
nearly a Vet

Outback Adventure

Puffin Books

Juliet
nearly a
Vet

Outback Adventure

REBECCA JOHNSON
Illustrated by Kyla May

Puffin Books

PUFFIN BOOKS

UK | USA | Canada | Ireland | Australia
India | New Zealand | South Africa | China

Penguin Books is part of the Penguin Random House group of companies
whose addresses can be found at global.penguinrandomhouse.com.

Penguin
Random House
PENGUIN BOOKS

First published by Penguin Group (Australia), 2015

Cover and text design by Karen Scott © Penguin Group (Australia)
Illustrations by Kyla May Productions
Typeset in New Century Schoolbook
Colour separation by Splitting Image Colour Studio, Clayton, Victoria
Printed and bound in Australia by Griffin Press, an accredited ISO AS/NZS 14001
Environmental Management Systems printer.

National Library of Australia
Cataloguing-in-Publication data:

Johnson, Rebecca.
Outback Adventure/Rebecca Johnson; illustrated by Kyla May.

ISBN: 978 0 14 330871 3 (pbk.)

A823.4

puffin.com.au

MIX
Paper from
responsible sources
FSC® C009448

Hi! I'm Juliet. I'm ten years old.
And I'm nearly a vet!

I bet you're wondering how someone who is only ten
could nearly be a vet. It's pretty simple really.
My mum's a vet. I watch what she does and
I help out all the time. There's really not that
much to it, you know...

For Robyn Sheahan-Bright, Clare Forster and Lisa Riley. Thank you for seeing a future in Juliet when she was nearly a novel.

XX R

CHAPTER 1

Sometimes vets need to travel

I'm sitting on my suitcase trying to get it shut when Mum pops her head into my room.

'Nearly ready to go, love?' she says. 'We need to leave for the airport in a few minutes.'

'Coming,' I say.

I open up my case and make a quick decision. My vet kit *does* take up a lot of room in my suitcase, but there's no way I'm leaving it behind. I pull out three T-shirts to make more room and finally manage to zip the suitcase up.

I put all my T-shirts on, one over the top of the other, and drag my suitcase towards the front door. I bump into Dad on the way. He squints at me and shakes his head.

'Juliet, how many layers are you wearing? You're going to boil on the plane, let alone when we get to Longreach. You know how hot it gets out there. Put them in your suitcase.'

'I can't.'

'What do you mean you can't?' Dad starts to reach out towards my case and I panic. If he sees my vet kit in there, he'll go bananas.

I step in front of my case. I have to

think quickly. 'I can't . . . stand to be cold. Last time we went, it was freezing on the plane.'

Dad rolls his eyes and shakes his head. 'Juliet, it is absolutely *not* going to be cold.'

Mum comes in dragging Max's case. I'm sure I can see the outline of a dinosaur under the canvas and Max has a pterodactyl in his hand.

'Please tell me you are not taking a suitcase full of dinosaurs, Max,' says Dad.

'But Jack is bringing his. He loves dinosaurs too. And my pterodactyl wants to see how it feels to really fly.'

My cousin Jack is seven years old

and he and Max spend ages on the phone talking about dinosaurs. I wish Aunty Sophie had a daughter that loved animals. Jarrod is nine and close to my age, but he hates animals. I don't think he likes me very much either.

'I've checked Max's case and he's got everything he needs,' says Mum. 'Have you got everything, Juliet?'

'Sure do,' I say, as we hear Chelsea and her mum call out, 'Hello,' from the front steps.

I race down to give Mrs O'Sullivan the lists I've made for her, so she'll know how to look after our dog Curly, my six chickens and our two guinea

pigs while we're away. She seems a
little surprised as she looks at the four
pages of instructions. When I pass her
the guinea pigs' grooming kit her eyes
go wide. I think she must be excited —
I can understand that. Vets know
how much fun it is to look after other
people's animals.

Chelsea is beside herself because
this is her first trip to the outback
and her first time on a plane. She says
goodbye to her mum and I give Curly
some extra hugs before Dad hurries us
into the car and we are off.

Chelsea loves flying as much as I do. We
share the window and look down at the

land changing below us. After we take off from Brisbane there's a lot of green, but as we get closer to Longreach, there's nothing but flatness and dry-looking dirt with the odd gum tree.

'I don't think I've ever seen it so dry,' I hear Mum say to Dad. 'No wonder they're struggling to feed the cattle.'

As we come in to land, we fly over some dams with only a little water left in them. I can see the tracks of cattle and sheep around the edges. They look like little puddles surrounded by polka dots.

'Look!' says Chelsea, as the plane gets even lower. A large mob of kangaroos is bounding away from the

noise of the plane. 'We're really in the
outback now!'

The first thing that hits me as we
leave the airport terminal is the heat.
I can't stand wearing all my T-shirts
for a minute longer and start stripping
them off.

Dad is about to put my case in the

hire car when he sees me tying the last of the T-shirts around my waist.

Before I have a chance to stop him, Dad unzips my suitcase to put them in. His mouth falls open when he sees my vet kit, taking up more than half the space.

'Juliet! What's your vet kit doing in here? Where are all your clothes?'

'They're in there,' I say. 'You just can't see them. I needed my vet kit in case there was an emergency.'

'The only emergency around here is going to be you!' snaps Dad.

We finish loading our stuff into the car and drive towards the town centre. Dad doesn't look happy.

'Look at that!' yells Max, startling us all. His face is pressed against the window.

Dad slows down as we pass a horse-drawn carriage. It's loaded up with people and has two men sitting on the front guiding the four horses.

'I can't believe some people don't have cars out here,' says Chelsea.

'They have cars, Chelsea,' says Mum. 'That's just a carriage people can ride on to see how everyone got around in the past. It's one of the original mail coaches.'

'It's beautiful,' says Chelsea, smiling. 'I'd love to go to school in that.'

'But that's *not* what I was looking at,'

Max blurts out. 'There was a big sign back there with a *dinosaur* on it. Do they still have those here as well?'

'That's a new sign for the dinosaur museum at Winton, Max,' says Dad. 'I thought you and Jack might like to go there one day. They don't have any living dinosaurs, but they've got heaps of real dinosaur bones and fossils.'

'Wow!' says Max, bouncing up and down on the seat in excitement.

Chelsea and I shake our heads. It's ridiculous how excited Max gets over dinosaurs.

I open my wallet to look at a picture of Curly. I wonder how he's going without us.

CHAPTER
2

Vets are problem solvers

'I just want to stop in town and get some flowers for Grandma before we head out to the property,' says Mum.

Dad drives into the main street of Longreach and we all wait in the car while Mum goes into the florist.

All the cars are really dusty and lots of people are wearing jeans and boots and dirty work clothes. I'm quite sure it won't matter if I have to wear the same clothes more than once. I remember why I like this place so much.

After a while we hear Mum tap
on the back hatch of the car and Dad
pushes the button to open it.

Suddenly I see Dad's eyes grow
huge in the rear-view mirror and he
starts to jump around in his seat,
trying to get his seatbelt off and turn
around at the same time.

'Dad, what is it?' I say.

'Emu,' Dad squeaks.

Chelsea, Max and I all turn around.
There's an emu at the back of the car
with its head poking inside!

Chelsea and Max scream and start
diving over the seat to be in the front
with Dad. Max is crying. Or Dad is.
I can't actually tell, because I don't

want to take my eyes off the emu.

We stare at each other for a moment. The emu has big brown eyes with long, wispy lashes. The top of its head is covered in little feathers that stand up on their ends and it has a wide, grey, pointed beak. It makes a low drumming noise with its throat.

'It's adorable,' I whisper.

Carefully, I reach into my backpack and pull out a half-eaten sandwich from the plane.

'Are you hungry?' I ask, as I slowly unwrap the food, out of sight of the emu. I carefully open my window and throw the sandwich off to the side of the car as far as I can.

The emu whips its head out and races towards the treat on the ground. I leap out of the other side of the car and run to the back to slam the hatch down. Then I jump back into the car.

Dad, Chelsea and Max all just stare at me in silence.

Eventually, Chelsea says, 'And that is why she's nearly a vet.'

❖

Mum comes back to the car to find three people in the front seat. We all start talking at once. She's very confused by all the commotion.

'There was a huge emu . . .' says Max. 'Juliet saved us.'

Dad tells Mum the whole story. She listens and nods, but doesn't seem very surprised.

'They're coming into town because they're hungry and thirsty from the drought. They can be a bit frightening, can't they, Max?'

He nods and Mum gives him a hug

before he and Chelsea hop back in
next to me.

Just as we're about to go, we hear it
again. *Tap. Tap. Tap.*

The emu is back at the rear window.

'He thinks we'll feed him more,'
says Mum, 'but he needs to go and find
some emu food, not human food.'

Dad carefully backs the car up and
we all watch the emu slowly step out
of the way. He's beside the car now and
Max holds his pterodactyl up to the
window. The emu pecks at it through
the glass and Max starts to laugh.

The emu follows us as we slowly
head down the main street. A few
people laugh and point as they see the

line of cars with the emu tucked right in behind ours.

Dad turns the corner and so does the emu. We're all laughing now.

'Go faster, Dad, go faster!' yells Max, and Dad starts to accelerate as we head for the open road. The emu jogs along behind us with his wings flapping up and down with each step. As we speed up so does he.

'Look how fast he can run!' Chelsea says.

I whip out my Vet Diary. I want to start a page on emus right away.

'How fast *can* they run, Mum?' I say.

'Well, they say emus can run at nearly fifty kilometres per hour.'

'Well, we're doing forty now,' says
Dad. 'Let's see how he goes!'

Dad speeds up a little more and
the emu races along beside us. We
wind down the windows and can hear
his feet make a sound like a galloping
horse. Max cheers him on, holding the
pterodactyl in the air.

'I think that's enough for him now,' says Dad, and he speeds up to leave the emu behind us.

'It's sad that they're so hungry and thirsty,' I say, starting on my notes.

'They're not too badly off,' says Mum. 'They come into town to drink in the dry times and they eat the grass from people's lawns.'

'I'd love a pet emu!' says Max.

Dad shudders at the thought of an emu eating his front lawn.

CHAPTER 3

Vets love the outback

We drive for another two hours, which gives me heaps of time to update my Vet Diary with what Mum has told me about emus. The road is so straight and flat it makes it easy to write.

FACTS ABOUT EMUS:

- Emus can run at nearly fifty kilometres per hour.

- They use their wings to balance as they run.

- An emu's diet is mainly grass and seeds.

- Emus cannot fly.

When I look out the window, I see dry, open land. Max has fallen asleep with dinosaurs all over his lap, but Chelsea and I want to look out the window for outback animals. We want to see as many as we can.

There are some poor, dead kangaroos beside the road that have been hit by cars and trucks, but we see lots of live ones too, bounding away when they hear the sound of the car.

'We're here,' says Dad finally.

We look up to see a sign over a large gate with a cattle grid.

'Sunnyside Station,' I read aloud. 'This is where my grandparents live, Chelsea.'

Chelsea looks around at the dry, dusty paddock.

'Um, Juliet,' she whispers, brushing a bit of dust off her crisp, white top. 'They do live in a house, don't they?'

Mum has overheard her. 'It's about three more kilometres from here to the house,' she says.

Chelsea can't believe it. 'Three kilometres from the front gate to the front door,' she says, sounding amazed.

We drive along the bumpy driveway towards the homestead. Mum must be really excited to see her parents. It's been almost a year since we've seen them or our cousins.

Suddenly a trail bike rides up beside

us. I wave like crazy when I realise it's Grandpa. Dad stops the car and we all pile out. Everyone's hugging each other. Grandpa can't believe how much we've grown.

'Grandpa, this is Chelsea,' I say. 'She's nearly a world-famous animal trainer and groomer and she's my best friend.'

'Well, nice to meet you, Chelsea. I can always use a new station hand.'

Grandpa looks over at Max. 'Anyone want a ride to the house on the motorbike? I've just radioed Grandma to ask her to put the kettle on.'

'Me!' says Max, jumping about. Grandpa grabs the spare helmet and puts it on Max's head and Dad helps him

climb onto the back of the motorbike.
Max is grinning from ear to ear.

We follow them up the long driveway.

'Hello, hello!' cries Grandma as she
comes rushing out to meet us and give
us all a hug. 'You must be hungry after
such a big trip,' she says. 'Who's ready
for some afternoon tea?'

Dad's eyes light up. He loves Grandma's cooking.

We take our bags inside and have some yummy homemade biscuits, then Max and I show Chelsea around the farmhouse and the yard.

'Over here are Grandma's chooks and that's her house cow, Creamy.

They milk her every morning and night. We'll be able to help.'

Chelsea looks at Creamy's bulging udder and long teats and pulls a face. 'Maybe I'll just watch.'

'You'll want to have a go, trust me,' I say. 'It's hilarious. Once Grandpa squirted Max in the face with the milk.'

Max kills himself laughing at the memory. Chelsea screws up her nose, but I know she's going to love it.

'They also have a cat called Ratter, but he's usually in the barn catching mice. He's not super friendly, but I'm sure you'll be able to fix that.'

Chelsea nods in agreement. 'Why are those dogs tied up over there?'

'They're the working dogs,' says Max. 'Grandpa uses them to help move the cattle and sheep, but they stay tied up when they're not working so they keep out of trouble.'

Suddenly a car horn toots. My cousins have arrived. Max runs around to the front yard, but I take another look around me. I love being in the outback surrounded by all these animals. I just hope Jarrod doesn't make fun of me this time.

CHAPTER
4

Some people don't like vets

Everyone's talking in the kitchen when
we come inside.

Uncle Stan and Aunty Sophie give
me a huge hug. I introduce them to
Chelsea, but something makes me
stop before I tell them she's nearly
world-famous.

Jarrod's sitting at the table eating
biscuits.

'Hello, Jarrod,' I say. 'This is Chelsea.'

'Hi, Juliet, not even a vet,' mumbles
Jarrod, a little too quietly for any of the

adults to hear. He just smirks at us.

Chelsea and I look at each other and she frowns. I did try to warn her about my cousin Jarrod.

'We're going back outside,' I say.

'Jarrod, you should go outside with the girls,' says Grandpa. 'You can keep an eye out for snakes for them.'

Chelsea stops in her tracks.

'Don't worry about snakes, Chelsea,' I say. 'The dogs go nuts if there's a snake around.'

'I want to stay here,' moans Jarrod.

'Off you go, please,' says Uncle Stan.

'Stay in the house yard, Jarrod,' says Aunty Sophie. 'And look out for the girls.'

I can't help but roll my eyes as I walk out the door. I'm nearly a vet. I certainly don't need a babysitter looking out for me, and neither does Chelsea.

We go back into the yard. Jarrod follows along, but he doesn't speak to us.

'Let's collect the eggs, Chelsea,' I say.

'Are you coming in?' I ask Jarrod, as I hold the chook gate open.

'Nah. I hate chickens. They stink.'

Chelsea gasps.

'Fine,' I say, and I slam the gate shut.

The laying boxes have lots of eggs in them. I think Grandma might have left some there for us to collect.

'Jarrod, can you pass that bucket in, please? We can't carry all these eggs.'

He seems to think about whether he'll do it, then slowly wanders over to get the bucket under the washing line. He stands back about a metre from the pen and holds it out to me.

'Um, my hands are full of eggs,' I say. 'Can you bring it in?'

'I'm not going in there. I told you – it stinks.'

'I'll get it,' says Chelsea helpfully. She opens the gate to reach the bucket and a chook makes a charge for freedom.

'Yuck! Get away,' says Jarrod as it runs towards him.

I'm sure I see him try to kick the chicken.

'Hey!' yells Chelsea. 'It's never okay to be cruel.'

'Well, I told you I hate them! It shouldn't have come near me,' Jarrod yells back and storms inside.

Chelsea and I collect the rest of the eggs then gently round up the escaped chook and put her back in the pen. We both sniff her. She doesn't stink in the least.

We carry the eggs inside then go and find Max and Jack. They are in the end room unpacking their suitcases. Jack has brought just as many dinosaurs as Max.

'Hey, Juliet, look at this. Jack and I have the exact same diplodocus!

They're even the same colour.'

'That's amazing,' I say, wishing Jarrod liked me as much as Jack likes Max. I'm so glad Chelsea's here.

'Do you guys want to come to the barn with us?' I say.

'Yeah!' they say together.

'We're going to the barn to find Ratter,' I tell Mum on our way back out.

'Oh dear, is that a good idea?' says Aunty Sophie.

'Rachel and I grew up playing in that barn, honey. It's fine,' Uncle Stan reassures her.

Aunty Sophie doesn't look too sure. She grew up in the city and she doesn't go outside much when they come to the country to visit.

'You going too?' asks Uncle Stan, looking at Jarrod.

'No,' he says. 'I hate barns. They stink.'

Uncle Stan shakes his head. 'Maybe if you tried playing in one, you'd see how much fun they are.'

Jarrod gets up and goes off to his room.

Chelsea, Max, Jack and I head towards the back door.

'How could anyone not like barns?' I ask Chelsea when we enter the lovely coolness of the big shed.

She shakes her head and shrugs.

'Ratter,' she calls softly. 'Where are you?'

The boys have climbed up onto a tractor each and are pretending to race them.

'Hey, Jack,' I ask. 'Is Jarrod always so cranky?'

'No, not at home,' he says, jiggling around and bouncing up and down on the seat.

'Maybe it *is* just me?' I whisper to Chelsea.

CHAPTER 5

Vets love looking at animals

The back door slams and Grandpa comes out and starts putting on his boots. Chelsea and I have been outside for an hour looking for Ratter. Max and Jack are firing slingshots at an old lid nailed to a tree.

'Who's coming on the lick run to the eastern paddocks with me?' Grandpa calls across to the barn.

The boys race over straightaway. I see Chelsea hesitating.

'Coming?' I say.

'Um . . . I don't want to lick anything in a paddock. I can wait here.'

I laugh and give her a hug. 'Chelsea, a *lick* is the name for a mineral block the farmers put in the paddocks for the *cattle* to lick. It's really important in the outback when there's a drought and the cattle have nothing to eat.'

'Oh, thank goodness,' says Chelsea. 'I really didn't fancy licking anything out here, especially when it's so dry and dusty.'

I grab my Vet Diary from my back pocket to show Chelsea the page I did on cattle licks the last time we were here.

CATTLE LICKS:

- They give extra minerals or supplements that cows can't get from the paddock.

- They are called 'licks' because the cattle lick them to get the goodness from them.

- They are used a lot in droughts because there isn't enough other feed in the paddocks.

- They look like a big dog bowl with a lid over the top.

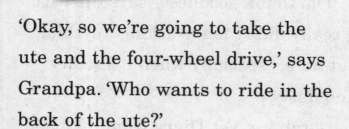

'Okay, so we're going to take the ute and the four-wheel drive,' says Grandpa. 'Who wants to ride in the back of the ute?'

'Meeee!' we all cheer together.

'And me,' says Mum as she pulls her boots on and joins us.

Uncle Stan is next out the door. 'Looks like I'm taking the four-wheel drive then.'

'Well, I'll keep Uncle Stan company,' says Dad as he joins us.

'Is Mum coming?' asks Jack.

'No, mate. She wants to stay and help Gran with dinner. Jarrod should be coming, though.'

We all turn to the door at the back of the house. There's no sign of Jarrod.

'I'll go get him,' says Uncle Stan with a sigh.

Suddenly I realise I might need my vet kit and race back into the house to get it. I know Jarrod will make fun of me, but vets always like to be prepared.

As I pass the room where Jarrod is, I hear Uncle Stan raising his voice a bit. 'I don't care if they stink. We haven't driven all this way for you to watch television!'

Quickly, I run to my room. I can't help wondering why Jarrod is being so difficult.

I'm back out in no time and lift my kit into the back of the ute. Grandpa has let the working dogs off their chains and they are running around our legs excitedly.

'Get down!' snaps Grandpa, and the dogs obediently drop to the ground. I can see that Chelsea is very impressed.

Uncle Stan comes back out of the house with Jarrod, who doesn't look at all pleased. He has his hand over his mouth and nose as if he's trying not to breathe.

'Here,' says Uncle Stan, holding the ute door open for him. 'You can ride up front with Grandpa.'

'Great,' says Grandpa. 'You can help me spot the dingoes.'

'Dingoes?' squeaks Chelsea. 'You didn't tell me there were dingoes!'

'Don't worry, Chelsea. Dingoes stay as far away from people as they can.'

I notice Jarrod walks around the front of the ute to get in and avoid the 'stinking' farm dogs.

We all sit down in the back tray on some large sacks of feed.

'Hold on tight and no standing up,' warns Mum.

The ute begins to slowly make its way along the worn dirt track that leads to the eastern paddocks. Each

time we come to a gate, Dad jumps out to open it for both vehicles to pass through. The dogs are racing through the paddocks like crazy.

'It's so dry,' says Mum sadly, as we stare out at the dry, red dirt. 'See where all of those scrubby mulga trees

have been pushed over?' she says, pointing. 'Grandpa and Grandma have to do that so the cattle can eat the leaves, because there's no grass.'

We come to our first water trough and Grandpa jumps out to check it.

'Where does the water come from?' says Max, looking around for a hose.

'They pump it up from deep under the ground,' Mum answers.

'I just hope they don't hit any dinosaur fossils when they dig down,' says Max.

Jack gasps at the thought.

Honestly, how does Max make *everything* about dinosaurs? He really does have a one-track mind.

We drive on a little further until we can see the cattle lick up ahead.

The cattle see us coming and start to walk in our direction. Some of the calves get excited and start to run, which makes their mothers run too.

Pretty soon we're being followed by lots of excited cattle. I must admit, I'm pretty excited too. Most vets would be.

CHAPTER
6

Vets need to pay attention.

'You kids stay in the ute,' says Mum, as she leaps off the back. Uncle Stan, Grandpa and Mum grab some bags of minerals for the lick.

Mum and Uncle Stan grew up around cattle. They push their way through them with no fear at all. I hope I'm that brave one day.

Some of the more curious cattle come right up to the ute and hang their heads over the sides. Chelsea and I reach out to pat them, but they pull back straightaway.

Both cars are surrounded by cattle pushing to get closer to the lick. I love their big, kind eyes and the sounds they make. I even like the smell of them.

I can see lots of calves that are about nine months old.

'See those calves, Chelsea?' I say, pointing. 'They need to be separated from their mothers so Grandma and Grandpa can wean them.'

'What does *wean* mean?' says Jack.

'Weaning is when a calf is made to stop drinking its mother's milk. If you don't wean them, some calves keep on drinking the milk and it can actually make the mother very unhealthy.

It's not good for the calf either.'

Jack looks at Max and seems to be pretty impressed.

'I told you she was nearly a vet,' says Max shrugging.

I turn around to look at the cattle that have gathered around the front of the ute and catch a glimpse of Jarrod on the front seat. He's curled in a ball with his hands over his head.

'Chelsea, I've just figured something out,' I whisper. 'Jarrod doesn't hate animals, he's *terrified* of them.'

I point to my cousin through the glass. Suddenly I feel really sorry for him.

'You know, Juliet,' whispers Chelsea. 'I don't think he hates *you* either.

Maybe he just hates that you're so brave with animals, because it makes him feel worse.'

No wonder Chelsea is nearly a world-famous animal trainer. She understands the way all kinds of animals think. Even the human kind!

'We have to find a way to help him, Chelsea,' I say.

After dinner, Uncle Stan and Grandpa make a campfire in the paddock next to the house.

We all sit around the fire on logs and listen as the adults talk about what needs to be done for the muster tomorrow. Grandma shows us how to

twist damper dough around sticks and
toast it in the fire. Then we dip it in
syrup and eat the warm bread under
a sky filled with stars. Grandpa pours
hot water from the billy into our mugs
and we tap our feet to the sound of
Uncle Stan strumming his guitar.

CHAPTER 7

Vets like being outside

The next morning we get up early. It's the cattle muster. Mustering days are always exciting. It's when the cattle are brought into the big yards to be checked, branded, tagged or wormed.

Today they will separate the grown-up calves from their mothers. Mum, Grandpa and Uncle Stan are going out to muster them, but we're not allowed to go because it can be dangerous if you don't know what you're doing. We'll be here to see the cattle as they come in though.

We wave Mum and the others goodbye as they head off on the trail bikes to round up the cattle.

Max and Jack have set up their dinosaurs in the barn. They're trying to lasso them with a thin rope. In a little while, they're going to drive to Winton with Aunty Sophie and Dad to see the dinosaur museum.

Jarrod is sitting on the lounge playing with his mum's phone. He doesn't want to go to the museum.

'I've got something special to show you three,' says Grandma after the others leave. 'I just need to do a couple of things before we go.'

I sit down next to Jarrod. Last
night, Chelsea and I talked about
how we might help him. Today's our
chance.

'Jarrod,' I say. 'We'd like to help you
with something.'

Jarrod stops playing his game on
the phone and looks at me. It's not a
very nice look, but I don't give up.

'Um, you know how you don't like
animals?'

'Because they stink,' he says.

'Well, yes . . . it's just that we
wondered if you *got to know* some
animals, maybe some small ones at
first and then some bigger ones, you

might see that they're really lovely. We could help you get to like them.'

'Why would I want to do that?' he sneers, and starts playing his game again.

Chelsea and I look at each other. Eventually Chelsea shrugs and we head outside.

When Grandma comes out with the washing, she has a small dish of mince balancing on top of the clothes.

'What's that for, Grandma?' I ask.

'Oh, you'll see,' she says with a smile.

Grandma taps her spoon on the side of her dish. Suddenly a chubby kookaburra flies down and lands on the washing line.

Grandma throws a little piece of mince into the air and the kookaburra catches it and scoffs it down.

'Oh, can we have a go?' I ask.

'Sure,' says Grandma.

Chelsea and I both throw little pieces of meat in the air for the kookaburra to catch, but we can't get them near enough to him and they keep landing on the grass.

'You need to throw it higher.' Jarrod is standing at the door looking out at us.

'We're trying,' says Chelsea, laughing.

Jarrod creeps down the stairs. I hold the bowl out to him and he tosses a small piece of meat in a perfect arc. The kookaburra gobbles it down happily.

We all laugh as Jarrod throws more pieces of mince for the kookaburra.

'Well, hello,' says Chelsea to the ginger cat who is now weaving around her legs. '*You* must be Ratter.'

'More like Ratbag,' says Grandma. 'Trust you to turn up when there is mince around.'

Chelsea picks Ratter up and puts him and the leftover mince on a bale of hay. The cat purrs loudly as it eats.

'Funny, he doesn't usually let strangers touch him,' says Grandma.

'Chelsea is very good with animals, Grandma,' I say. 'She's going to be a world-famous animal trainer and groomer one day.'

'Is that right?' says Grandma.

I notice that Jarrod has taken a step or two back towards the house.

'Jarrod,' I say. 'If Chelsea held Ratter, do you think you'd like to pat him?'

Jarrod doesn't move for a while. He opens his mouth as if to say something smart, but he closes it again.

Then he says, 'My mum doesn't like animals either.'

'Maybe she just hasn't had a chance to get to know one properly?' says Chelsea.

She scoops up the cat and walks towards Jarrod, but stops halfway. She sits on a upturned metal bucket and tickles the cat under the chin.

Jarrod takes a few steps towards Chelsea and looks down at the purring cat. 'Will it scratch me?' he asks.

'I don't think so,' says Chelsea. 'I can hold him a little tighter if you'd like to be sure.'

Jarrod nods slightly and Chelsea gently wraps her arms around the cat.

He slowly starts to pat Ratter – with just one finger at first, then his whole hand.

'I got bitten by a dog when I was little,' he says. 'Mum wouldn't let us have any animals after that. We live in an apartment, so we probably couldn't get one anyway.'

'I could tell you some good pets to keep in apartments,' I say. 'I have a page of them in my Vet Diary.'

Jarrod just shrugs his shoulders.

Grandma looks at me and then looks back at Jarrod stroking the cat. We smile at each other. I think she understands our plan.

'Would you like to pat Creamy? She's really gentle,' says Grandma. 'I could bring her over, close to the fence.'

Jarrod doesn't say no, so Grandma goes to get Creamy.

Once Grandma's tied Creamy to the other side of the wooden fence, we all walk over together. I notice Jarrod's hand is shaking as he reaches out to touch the cow through the fence.

'Try it like this,' I say, and show him how to pat in the direction the cow's hair goes in.

Soon Jarrod is softly patting Creamy. 'She's really smooth,' he says after a while.

Chelsea shows Jarrod her grooming kit and we comb and brush every inch of Creamy. Chelsea even finds a ribbon to tie in the cow's fringe.

'She looks wonderful!' Grandma smiles as we parade Creamy past the vegetable garden where she's working.

After we put Creamy back in her paddock, we sit on the back step with an icy pole and Jarrod tells us about his soccer team. It sounds like he's really good at soccer.

'So Jarrod, are you ready to meet a smelly chook now?' I say.

Chelsea and I both laugh when he smiles from ear to ear.

We start with a bantam chicken, like the ones I have at my house, and work our way up.

I pick out a small chicken for Jarrod to pat and soon he's hunting around in the chook pen for eggs with us. When I turn around I can't believe my eyes. He's actually holding a rooster!

'So who's ready to come for a drive with me to see something special?' says Grandma when we bring the eggs in.

We all jump into the four-wheel drive excitedly. My vet kit bumps around on the seat between Chelsea and me. Jarrod is sitting in the front seat with Grandma.

I tap Chelsea on the knee and point to a new list I'm making.

She smiles and gives me the thumbs up.

ANIMALS JARROD HAS MET:
- Kookaburras
- Cats
- Cows
- Chooks

CHAPTER
8

Vets like to help

We follow a different track to the
one from yesterday. This time we're
heading towards a gorge that lies
between two large groups of rocks.
Some corellas that have been looking
for seeds on the ground fly up in front
of us in a loud, dusty flock.

'Look over there!' says Chelsea,
pointing to some rock wallabies heading
for the safety of a large rocky outcrop.

Grandma slows down as we near the
rocks that sit either side of the gorge.

We climb down from the car and follow Grandma along a thin track that weaves between the large red-and-brown rocks. Together we enter a big, open cave.

It takes a minute for our eyes to adjust to the dim light, and then we see them: painted handprints and drawings cover the walls.

'Who did these?' I ask. 'They're beautiful.'

'The Iningai people are the traditional owners of this land. They ground up the rocks to make the paint to tell their stories,' says Grandma.

We stand and look for ages. I wonder about the stories behind these prints.

The silence is broken by a frantic, scratching sound from outside the cave.

I step outside to see if I can hear it again. It's coming from behind the next rock so I tiptoe closer.

Then I see – it's a frill-necked lizard! When it sees me, it puffs its frill up and hisses. It tries to run towards a tree a short distance away, but somehow a long strand of dry grass has looped around its neck and been caught under its rough scaly frill. The long grass is attached to a ball of tumbleweed, so wherever the lizard goes, the big ball of dead weed follows it. The weed keeps getting caught on rocks and things. The lizard pushes its

body up in a high arc and hisses again.

'What is it?' says Chelsea, from
behind me.

'It's a frill-necked lizard and it's in
trouble,' I say.

'Can you help it, Juliet?' asks Chelsea.

'I'm not sure that's a good idea,' says
Grandma. 'They can give a nasty bite.'

'We'll be careful, Grandma. We can't just leave it to die,' I say.

'Jarrod, can you please grab my vet kit from the car? Is there a blanket or towel in the car, Grandma?'

Grandma still looks a bit unsure, but Jarrod is back in an instant with the kit and an old jumper of Grandpa's.

'This is going to be a team effort,' I say, holding my hand out for the jumper. Jarrod throws it to me from as far back as he can stand.

I slowly put my foot on the tumbleweed. The lizard feels the movement and darts forward, but is quickly stopped as the grass pulls him back. As fast as I can, I throw the jumper over him and drop to my hands and knees, pinning the lizard under the material.

'Quick, Chelsea,' I say. 'Help me hold him down.'

Chelsea jumps into action, and together we have the frantic hissing lizard under control.

Jarrod is clearly gobsmacked.

'Can you pass me the scissors from my vet kit, Jarrod?' I ask.

He clicks the kit open and grabs the scissors then takes a few steps closer to pass them to me.

'I still don't think this is a good idea,' says Grandma. 'A lizard bite can get really infected.'

'Sometimes vets have to take risks, Grandma,' I say.

Grandma shakes her head and mutters something about what our parents would say.

'Chelsea and Jarrod, do you think you could hold him down while I try to snip this grass?'

'You hold his tail, Jarrod,' I say. 'I think I can get to his neck from the side here, without us having to uncover his head.'

It's a bit tricky to work around each other without letting the lizard go, but we manage to peel the side of the jumper up enough to see where the grass is caught.

'Hold him still,' I whisper as I edge my scissors in to do the job.

I snip the wiry grass and gently start to pull it free from around the lizard's neck.

Jarrod pulls the bunch of tumbleweed away from under the jumper.

'When I say go, we all need to jump back together. One, two, three, go!'

We all leap back as I pull the jumper off the hissing lizard. It darts forward and scurries up the nearest tree in seconds.

'Well, I never!' says Grandma.

'I guess that's why she's nearly a vet,' says Jarrod, smiling.

'I guess so,' says Grandma. 'We'd better hurry back now. The others will be back soon and a vet certainly wouldn't want to miss them bringing the cattle in.'

CHAPTER 9

Sometimes vets need help too

As we come back up the driveway we see a cloud of dust in the nearby paddocks. The muster is back!

'Come on, Chelsea and Jarrod,' I say when we pull up at the house. 'Let's sit up on the fence to watch them come in.'

We all climb up on the rails of the stockyards. The dogs are running like mad from side to side, keeping the cattle in a group.

The gates are open and the cattle head towards us with hooves pounding the dry earth. Uncle Stan cracks his whip high above their heads.

'I've never seen so many cows!' yells Chelsea over the noise of the herd and the motorbikes. More and more cattle are driven into the huge holding paddock. They'll stay there until the calves can be separated from their mothers.

We wave to Mum and Uncle Stan and Grandpa. I look behind me as one of the dogs shoots under the fence barking. Suddenly, I lose my balance and fall heavily onto the ground inside the yard.

'Juliet!' screams Chelsea.

I'm winded and can't get up. The terrified faces of Jarrod and Chelsea look down from above me.

I can see the strong brown legs of
a thousand cattle coming thundering
towards me and I start to cry.

Suddenly, Jarrod jumps down beside
me and waves his arms madly at the
cattle, yelling, 'Get back! Get back!'

He pulls me up by the arm and
helps me climb over the fence to
Chelsea. I'm shaking as I fall onto the
grass on the other side of the fence.
Jarrod clambers over after me.

Uncle Stan and Grandpa have
seen what's happening, and they leap
off their motorbikes and rush over
towards us.

'Are you all right, love?' says Uncle
Stan, helping to steady me.

Chelsea is busily brushing the dust off my clothes.

I nod and try to smile at him, but I'm still very shaken.

'Well,' says Grandpa, giving Jarrod a pat on the back, 'you were very brave there young man. You're nearly a cattleman by the looks of you!'

Jarrod smiles and Uncle Stan ruffles his hair.

I give Jarrod a huge hug. Vets love working with cattlemen.

Later that night as we all sit by the campfire again, I show Jarrod my list of the animals he's met and he beams when he sees the last entry.

ANIMALS JARROD HAS MET:
- Kookaburras
- Cats
- Cows
- Chooks
- Angry frill-necked lizards
- Charging cattle

'Can I keep this, Juliet?' he says. 'I'd like to add to it and post it back to you one day.'

'Sure you can,' I say as I tear it from my Vet Diary.

'And could I have that list of animals that can live in apartments, too?' he says.

The look on Aunty Sophie's face when she hears this makes us all burst out laughing.

I can't wait to show Jarrod how to set up his apartment for a pet of his own!

Quiz! Are You Nearly a Vet?

1. A group of kangaroos is called a:
    a. Flock
    b. Herd
    c. Mob
    d. Bound

2. The most important thing for a vet to take on holidays is their:
    a. Toothbrush
    b. Pyjamas
    c. Jumper
    d. Vet kit

3. Emus can run at speeds up to:
    a. 50 km/h
    b. 500 km/h
    c. 5 km/h
    d. 5000 km/h

4. Which of these things are not used to round up cattle?
    a. Helicopters
    b. Horses
    c. Motorbikes
    d. Skateboards

5. A 'lick' is used to give extra nutrients to the:
    a. Cattle
    b. Farmer
    c. Working dogs
    d. Chooks

6. To 'wean' means to stop a mammal from drinking:
a. Cordial
b. Milk
c. Water
d. Juice

7. What do you do with a whip?
a. Twist it
b. Crack it
c. Poke it
d. Wriggle it

8. Frill-necked lizards cannot:
a. Climb trees
b. Run fast
c. Bite
d. Spit poison

9. When farmers round up cattle they call it a:
a. Party
b. Muster
c. Stampede
d. Stockyard

10. What sort of noise do emus make?
a. Gurgle
b. Drumming
c. Screech
d. Cluck

The Great Pet Plan

My best friend Chelsea and I ♥ animals.
I have a dog Curly and two guinea pigs, but
we need more pets if I'm going to learn to be
a vet. Today, we had the best idea ever...
We're going to have a pet sleepover!

At the Show

Chelsea and I are helping our friend, Maisy,
get her pony ready for the local show. But
Midgie is more interested in eating than in
learning to jump (sigh). Pony training is a bit
more difficult than we thought!

Farm Friends

It's Spring and all the animals on Maisy's farm
are having babies. Maisy says I can stay for a
whole week and help out. There are chicks and
ducklings hatching, orphan lambs to feed, and
I can't wait for Bella to have her calf!

Bush Baby Rescue

A terrible bushfire has struck and Mum's vet clinic is in chaos. Every day more and more injured baby animals arrive. Chelsea and I have never been busier! But who knew that babies needed so much feeding. I may never sleep again!

Beach Buddies

It's the holidays and we're going camping by the beach. I can't wait to toast marshmallows by the campfire, swim in the sea and explore the rock pools – there are so many amazing animals at the beach.

Zookeeper for a Day

I've won a competition to be a zookeeper for a day! My best friend Chelsea is coming too. I can't wait to learn all about the zoo animals. There will be meerkats, tigers and penguins to feed. And maybe some zoo vets who need some help (I won't forget my vet kit!).

The Lost Dogs

There was a huge storm last night and now there are lots of lost dogs. One turned up outside my window (he must have known I'm nearly a vet). Luckily, Chelsea, Mum and I are helping out at the Lost Dogs' Home.

Playground Pets

Chelsea and I have such a cool school – we get to have playground pets! Guinea pigs, lizards, fish and insects are all part of our science room. But this week, we have a replacement teacher, and Miss Fine doesn't know much about animals. Luckily we do (it's so handy being nearly a vet).

Outback Adventure

It's hot and dry in the outback where my grandparents live. I wonder what outback animals we'll see? My cousin Jarrod will be there, but I get the feeling he doesn't like me very much and – even worse – he doesn't seem to like animals! Maybe this is my chance to change his mind . . .

Cat Show Queen

REBECCA JOHNSON

There's a cat show in town and some of the cats are
going to board at Mum's vet clinic. Chelsea and I can't
wait to see all the different types of cats. All the owners
have special techniques for preparing their pets for
the show – and some are very fussy. When there's a
cat-astrophe, its lucky that my best friend is almost a
world-famous animal trainer and groomer!

From Rebecca Johnson

I've never actually been to Longreach, so when I wrote
this book I had to try to find out as much as I could
about it. I took my chances and started randomly
ringing people who lived there to ask them to describe
some things for me. I was very lucky to find a station
owner called Leone from a working cattle station
called Sunnyside. She was a fantastic help, giving me
so much detail about the hard work that comes with
a drought. What people say about country folk being
helpful certainly seems to be true. I am definitely
going to visit Longreach sometime!

From Kyla May

As a little girl, I always wanted to be a vet. I had
mice, guinea pigs, dogs, goldfish, sea snails, sea
monkeys and tadpoles as pets. I loved looking after
my friends' pets when they went on holidays, and
every Saturday I helped out at a pet store.
Now that I'm all grown up, I have the best job in
the world. I get to draw lots of animals for children's
books and for animated TV shows. In my studio
I have two dogs, Jed and Evie, and two cats,
Bosco and Kobe, who love to watch me draw.